For my nephew, Graham
—M. G.

Text and illustrations copyright © 1998 by Michael Garland
All rights reserved

Published by Caroline House
Boyds Mills Press, Inc.
A Highlights Company
815 Church Street
Honesdale, Pennsylvania 18431

Publisher Cataloging-in-Publication Data
Garland, Michael.
Angel cat / by Michael Garland.—1st.ed.
[32]p. : col. ill. : cm.
Summary: A cat returns from heaven to rescue her owners.
ISBN 1-56397-726-5
1. Cats—Fiction—Juvenile literature. 2. Angels—Fiction—Juvenile literature.
[1. Cats—Fiction. 2. Angels—Fiction.] I. Title.
[E]—dc21   1998   AC   CIP
Library of Congress Catalog Card Number 97-78119

First edition, 1998
Book designed by Tim Gillner and Michael Garland
The text of this book is set in 17-point Usherwood Book.
The illustrations were done electronically.

10 9 8 7 6 5 4 3 2 1

Reprinted by arrangement with Boyds Mills Press.
Printed in the U.S.A.

Angel Cat

MICHAEL GARLAND

BOYDS MILLS PRESS

The leaves blowing on the breeze were every shade of red, yellow, and orange. Matthew and Gillian played with their cats Yang and Yin, while Mom and Dad raked the leaves into great colorful mountains. It was a good day for making the most of the last warm weather.

Then something bad happened. Yin was crossing the road. She forgot to look both ways.

They buried Yin under the old maple tree behind the house.
Though the sun was shining, everyone felt gloomy, especially Yang.
　　Matthew asked Mom, "Where is Yin now?"
　　"She's in heaven."
　　"Is she an angel?" Gillian asked.
　　"Yes," said Mom. "Yin is an angel now."
　　That made Matthew and Gillian feel a little better.

Autumn faded into winter. The days grew shorter and colder. Matthew and Gillian still missed Yin very much. So did Yang.

Then something strange happened.

Yang began rolling and jumping and playing, just like he and Yin had always done together.

The children saw Yang do other strange things. His head would flit from side to side, his eyes would dart up and down, his tail would twitch, and his whiskers would stand straight up. It was as though Yang was watching a bird or a butterfly fluttering around the room . . . but there was nothing there.

It was a mystery why Yang seemed so distracted. Sometimes when Yang behaved this way, Matthew thought he could feel a faint breeze on his face. When he would ask Gillian if she felt it too, she would say, "I don't feel anything."

The winter came and covered the hills with a blanket of snow. When the sun dipped below the hills, the chilly day turned into an even chillier night. Icicles hung from the roof of the house, but at its heart, the fireplace was blazing. The fire warmed the house and the family as well.

Long into the night, all was silent except for a tick-ing clock and the quiet rhythm of sleeping sounds.

The fire in the fireplace seemed to be asleep too. Only a few embers sent a thin trail of smoke drifting up the chimney. That's when it happened.

POP! A spark burst out and landed on the fringe of the living-room rug.

There was no one around to see the spark glow and smolder. There was no one around to see the smoke rise from the little flame. No one except Yin. She flew around the room, invisible, frantic. Her angel cat wings beat furiously—up and down, back and forth. Yin knew what she had to do.

Yin flew upstairs into the parents' room and pounced on their bed. She clawed at the covers and flapped her wings in their faces. Nothing could stir them. Mom and Dad were too deep in their dreams to be awakened by an angel.

Yin flew into Gillian's room. But Gillian was sound asleep, too.

As clouds of smoke floated up to the second floor,
Yin fluttered and flapped her way to Matthew's room.
She jumped from dresser to desk and from desk to chair.
From the chair she jumped right down on Matthew's pillow.
Leaping, pouncing, scratching, nothing seemed to wake
the boy. Yin was about to meow her loudest "MEOW!"
right into Matthew's ear.

Before she could make a sound, her whiskers lightly touched Matthew's cheek. Matthew's nose twitched. His mouth crinkled. His eyes blinked and opened wide! Matthew stared in shock. Hovering before him was Yin, an angel cat, with angel cat wings and a glow that lit up the dark room.

Then Matthew could smell the creeping smoke. Yin flew from the room, into the hall and down the stairs. Matthew followed to the top step. He saw the flames on the edge of the rug below. He ran to wake his parents and Gillian. The family hurried down the stairs to the front door. Matthew, Gillian, their mother, and Yang went out just before Dad dragged the burning rug through the front door and onto the snow.

The fire was over. Only the rug was damaged. One look at their parents' faces and the children knew they were lucky to have escaped a disaster. They all went back inside and cleaned up. They opened the windows and let in fresh air. Dad replaced the dead battery in the smoke alarm.

With all the rush and confusion, Matthew didn't have a chance to tell about Yin and how he woke up. When he did, they laughed. They said he was dreaming.

Gillian said, "Where is Yin now? I don't see her! Where's the proof?"

Matthew didn't know how or why. He just knew what he saw.

Yang sat on the windowsill in the kitchen and looked out.
His tail started to swing back and forth. He could see Yin soaring
through the night air over the snowy yard. Her glowing light made
streaks as she flew higher into the dark blue sky, until finally she was
just another sparkle lost in the stars.